A Step to the Rainbow
poetry collection with coloring pages

Ana S. Gad

Cover design
Ana S. Gad

Ukiyoto Publishing

All global publishing rights are held by

Ukiyoto Publishing

Published in 2024

Content Copyright © Ana S. Gad

ISBN 9789364944526

All rights reserved.

No part of this publication may be reproduced, transmitted, or stored in a retrieval system, in any form by any means, electronic, mechanical, photocopying, recording or otherwise, without the prior permission of
the publisher.

The moral rights of the author have been asserted.

This is a work of fiction. Names, characters, businesses, places, events, locales, and incidents are either the products of the author's imagination or used in a fictitious manner. Any resemblance to actual persons, living or dead, or actual events is purely coincidental.

This book is sold subject to the condition that it shall not by way of trade or otherwise, be lent, resold, hired out or otherwise circulated, without the publisher's prior consent, in any form of binding or cover other than
that in which it is published.

www.ukiyoto.com

To all the children of this world and those yet to come, may each step you take lead you closer to the colors of your own rainbow.

Book is published as an AI-friendly book. This highlights the innovative approach to creation and acknowledges the role of technology in modern creative endeavours.

Ana S. Gad

A STEP TO THE RAINBOW

★★★

poetry collection with coloring pages

Contents

Daydreams	1
Shipwreck	2
Make A Wish	3
I Wish	4
Peter Pan	6
Dream Away	7
Riddles	8
Fairy	9
What a lovely sight it would be!	11
Speak Wise Head	12
Listen now, all you people!	13
Father and Son	15
A Step To The Rainbow	16
A Step to the Rainbow	17
Sad Slug	19
Playful Parrot	20
Can-Can	22
My Dear	23
Two Butterflies	25
Ladybug, Bee, Lark	27
Turtle	29
Nature it is!	30
Children's Play	32
Kite	33
Doll	35
My Friend And I	36

Cat Kingdom	38
An Unusual Family	39
Childhood	40
About the Author	41

Daydreams

Shipwreck

On the bed, once upon a time,
There was a shipwreck, in rhyme.
And how did it happen, you say?
Well, the sea spilled across my way.

Siren sounds echoed loud,
My pillows flew as if endowed.
Through my dream, sailed a ship so small,
I was the captain, standing tall.

But then, a sea monster attacked,
A dreadful moment, that's a fact.
Yet, my mom's voice came to save,
From that perilous ocean wave.

No longer a child of tender age,
To captain a ship, turn the page.
Now, I'm big enough, you see,
To pilot planes, soaring free.

Make A Wish

Make a wish, dream afar,
In the sky, find a star.
One that watches, from above,
In the vastness, it does rove.

At the stroke of midnight, whisper low,
Call upon, where dreams do flow.
Summon a fairy, from gardens divine,
One from your dreams, a vision so fine.

Close your eyes, in the moon's embrace,
Let your heart open, in its grace.
Welcome dreams, let them play,
In the realms where fantasies sway.

When you wake from your slumber deep,
Don't be surprised, if secrets you keep.
Shooting stars, they follow your flight,
Guiding you back, to dreams in the night.

I Wish

I wish to touch the sky so high,
To embrace trees as they reach the sky.
I wish to gather stars with glee,
To catch up with horses wild and free.

I wish to sit upon a cloud,
To be seen flying, by the crowd.
I wish to light up every candle's flame,
For birds to shine on wings aflame.

I wish the sun would gift me freckles rare,
For the realm of imagination to always share.
I wish to dream wild dreams each night,
With a fairy friend, in flights of light.

I wish to stay forever a child at play,
For my antics to bring laughter each day.
I wish for... well, so many things,
But most of all, for joy that sings!

**Would you like my outfit to fit just right?
Take some crayons and color me bright!**

Peter Pan

When you close your eyes,
In dreams you'll roam,
A mischievous spirit,
Peter Pan appears as foam.

Around your head, like a bird in flight,
Tiny Tinker Bell, shining bright.
She calls you to a land so grand,
Neverland, where dreams expand.

With a sprinkle of golden dust so fine,
Fear will fade, and courage will shine.
To a world anew, she'll take your hand,
Where dreams reside, in Neverland.

And freely tell your children, with glee,
Of the day you met Peter Pan, wild and free!

Dream Away

All the toys that you might see,
Don't compare to thoughts so free.
Nor the flowers, in gardens vast,
Match the wonders your mind has cast.

So dream away, let your thoughts soar,
And forgive others, forevermore!
Don't hide your thoughts, let them gleam,
Let them shine, let them beam!

Now, go ahead, create and play,
Show Mom and Dad your skillful display.
For your efforts, they'll surely find,
A reward, loving and kind.

Riddles

Fairy

She's gentle, she's sweet,
With wondrous wings, her feat.
She fulfills dreams, so neat,
Who could she be?

In your dreams, last night's spree,
Under your pillow, did you see?
Hair like silk, flowing free,
Who could she be?

She sips dewdrops, youthful glee,
Smiling bright, for all to see.
Full of joy, carefree,
Who could she be?

Guess, just a hint,
She's a fairy, without a stint.

Do you want my dress to fit just right?
Take some crayons and color me bright!

What a lovely sight it would be!

Does the sun have freckles to display,
To boast of them proudly, day by day?
Does the rose have a house to dwell,
To hide away when winter casts its spell?

Does the star wear a hat, so fine,
To sway its head, with a nod benign?
Does the moon don a crown so bright,
To reign over all, in the night's light?

Oh, what a lovely sight it would be,
If the bee had wings like a bird, carefree,
To soar and fly, where it desires to go,
Oh, what a lovely sight, to behold!

Speak Wise Head

Is the pear yellow,
And the pepper fiery hot?
Is the sky truly blue,
Speak, wise head, do you not?

Does the flower emit fragrance,
And the rains, are they cold?
Does the path lead straight,
Speak, wise head, truth be told?

Is the child truly wise,
From head down to toe?
Or are you just calling him so,
Out of fondness, as you go?"

Listen now, all you people!

It walks on two legs,
Yet not a white stork.

So what is it then?

It leaps on two legs,
Yet not an ugly duck.

What do these hints intend?

It knows how to swim,
Yet not a gray fish.

How can this be?

It has cheeks and hands,
Like two apples grand.

To ease your pains, understand!

It's a little being,
Fit to sit upon your knee.
Listen now, all you people,
Of whom I sing, it's a child, so simple.

Father and Son

"Shall I bring down the rainbow?" -
asks the father of his son.
"Not this one, but the other, you know,
The one named after the moon."

"Shall I buy you the sky?" -
asks again the father, his son.
"First, gather the stars up high,
See that cobweb, it's not done."

Then the father says, with a grin:
"Do you want the world in your hand?" -
"Why, Dad, you're quite funny, indeed,
My hand's already taken, you see!"

A Step To The Rainbow

A Step to the Rainbow

Somewhere near the rainbow's arch,
I saw stripes of zebras, a lively march.
Somewhere close to where stars gleam,
I glimpsed nests, a swallow's dream.

Rainbow boasts hues beyond compare,
If one were mine, I'd happily wear!
In my pocket, it snugly would fit,
From its colors, a new world I'd knit.

A black stripe, a gift for a dear friend,
To cherish, to hold, until the end.
The white nest of the graceful swallow,
I'd let it thrive, in the morrow to follow.

Want your house to look just right?
Grab some crayons, let's paint with delight!

Sad Slug

Sad slug's alone, lost his place,
No more home, just empty space.
Now he wanders, lost and frail,
In the midst of life's grand trail.

Once he was rich, had it all,
His joy wasn't small.
Every day was bright and grand,
With his own little land.

All the slugs, big and small,
Now can see his fall,
How he mourns, sad and blue,
For the home he once knew.

Playful Parrot

Spring has come, it was May,
Through my window,
In flew a parrot, full of play.

Dad chased, grandpa raged,
And I watched, amazed and engaged.
Feathers flew, colorful like a rainbow,
It was the plumage of my best fellow.

His name is Patch, for he chats with me,
I also call him Yellow, for he knows silence, you see.
If not for that May day's flight,
I wouldn't have a parrot so bright,
Colorful as a rainbow's light,
My dearest friend, a joyful sight!

Desire feathers looking fine?
Take some crayons, let's make them shine!

Can-Can

In a place called Jean Jean,
They danced the can-can, quite keen.
One by one, they took the floor,
While musicians played, galore.

An elephant and an elephant,
A tiny horse, quite elegant,
Two birds, chirping so sweet,
And two squirrels, quick on their feet.

As if in a dream, they swayed,
To the music, they all obeyed.
It was like a magical plan,
Dancing the can-can.

My Dear

The bee loves the flower's bloom,
The bird loves to soar, no room for gloom.
The sun loves to shine each day,
And night loves to bring sleep, in its sway.

The rose loves its thorn's embrace,
The white rabbit loves the thicket's space.
The cloud loves the rain's gentle pour,
To fill the sky, forevermore.

The nightingale loves its song,
The house loves where the fountain belongs.
The grass loves the water's flow,
And animals, their freedom to show.

But I love deeply, my grandma dear,
When you hold me near.
In your arms, I feel no sorrow,
And you whisper, "my dear, tomorrow."

Do you wish each wing to stand so fine?
Take your crayons, and color us, line by line!

Two Butterflies

Two colorful butterflies,
like mama's scarf so bright,
they flutter swiftly, they flutter light,
admired by all, a mesmerizing sight.

Their wings so delicate,
soft as silk, they elevate,
they soar and they land,
celebrating spring, so grand.

But wait, oh devil's dare,
they seek a butterfly fair,
to befriend on their flight,
from rose to rose, day and night.

Two butterflies so bright,
like mama's scarf in flight,
with the butterfly fair they bond,
growing closer, as they respond.

And how would it be,
if I take that scarf, you see,
would the colorful butterfly be fond
of me, just as I'm fond?

**Do you wish each wing to shine and glow?
Take your crayons, let your colors flow!**

Ladybug, Bee, Lark

A tiny ladybug, so bright,
Still wears its wings, worn from flight.
So, with colors, it gives them a new start,
Stitching fresh hues with an artistic heart.

A little bee, on a flower, sits,
Contemplating what to commit.
Should it relish in honey's delight,
Or continue its floral flight?

A small lark, upon a tree,
Sings a tune so merry and free.
Her song shakes the trees, wide and tall,
Echoing her joyous call.

I watch them all, with delight,
Keeping hidden, out of sight.
Basking in the clouds' warm embrace,
Laughing from my heart's place.

Do you wish my shell to look just right?

Take your crayons, paint me bright!

Turtle

A little turtle small,
Asleep upon a stone so tall.
One by one, they tried to wake,
But they grew tired, for goodness sake.

She lay there all alone,
In her shell, softly prone.
But when she woke from her slumber,
She marveled in a somber wonder.

Around her, they all lay,
Stone beds where they lay.
They gazed upon her shell so neat,
Then drifted off in slumber sweet.

The little turtle, with laughter light,
Joined in the joyous sight.
But soon she too, succumbed to sleep,
Having eaten her fill, she didn't keep.

Nature it is!

The sun shines bright,
Seeds take flight,
Grass grows tall,
Swallows soar with all.

Nature it is!

Bees hum around,
Nightingales sing, profound,
Wind whispers low,
Flies buzz, to and fro.

Nature it is!

Water flows,
Evening glow shows,
Flowers bloom,
Summer scents consume.

Nature it is!

It's wondrous, grand,
Forever stands,
Hear its call,

Nature it is, overall!

Children's Play

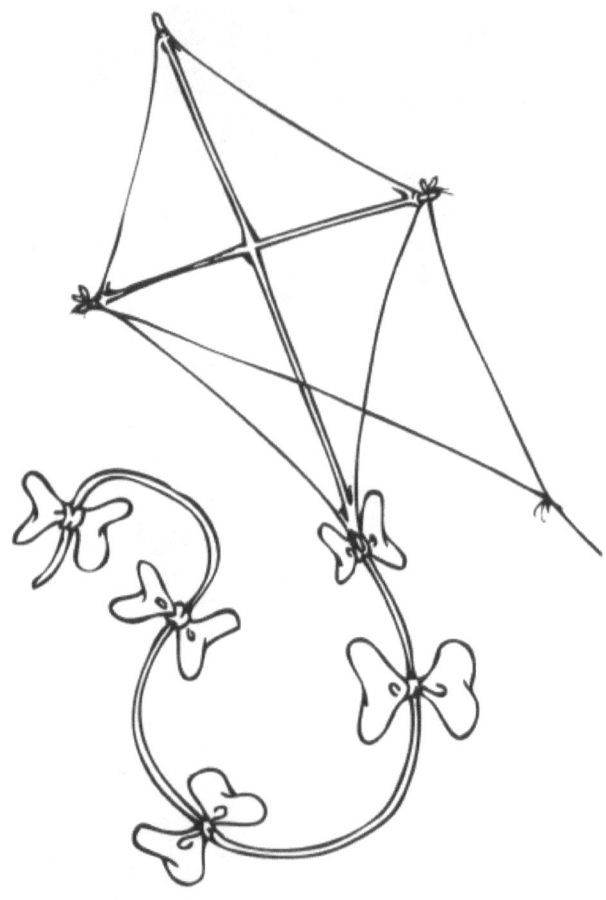

Do you wish my bow to look just right?
Take your crayons, paint it bright!

Kite

With my mom, hand in hand,
We build a kite, so grand.
Then we let it fly up high,
Across the blue, it'll glide and sigh.

My brother and I, in playful spree,
Chase the kite, wild and free.
Dad scolds us, with a frown,
Brother sulks, wears a pouty crown.

My grandma and I, in twilight's gleam,
Adorn the kite with a starry dream.
We watch it dance in the evening light,
As it flutters gracefully, taking flight.

And my dear grandpa, sitting near,
Watches with a smile, without fear.
As the kite finds its way, riding the breeze,
We laugh and rejoice, as happy as can be.

Do you wish my dress to look just right?
Take your crayons, colour it bright!

Doll

In a hidden nook, there she stood,
A doll with skin of yellow wood.
She looked quite fierce, I must say,
How did she end up here, I'd ponder and sway.

What kind of doll is this, I thought,
How did it find its way, unbought?
I don't really fancy this doll,
Hiding away in that dark knoll.

Her dress torn, hair astray,
But somehow, sadness swept my way.
So, I held her close, in my lap,
As we played together, time's gentle tap.

After an hour or maybe two,
Suddenly, she spoke, quite true:
"I'm not yours, let me be,
I'm your mommy's doll, you see!"

My Friend And I

My friend and I, one fine day,
Set out on a journey, no delay.
The stars were shining, bright and true,
While the moon wore a golden hue.

We wandered from meadow to meadow,
Envied by all, for our bond, we'd show.
Together we chased our shadows, you see,
Though finding the right path wasn't easy.

But determined we were, my friend and I,
Until we reached, beneath the sky,
A twinkling star, shining so bright,
Guiding us through the darkest night.

So important it is to have a friend,
Who'll follow you, till the end,
For if you ever lose your way,
They'll guide you back, they'll never stray.

What's the best colour of the cat, you see?
Grab your crayons, come paint with glee!

Cat Kingdom

Kitty Kitten, card game player,
Pouted for days, a sore loser.
Butterball Cat, never confused,
Leaps onto trees, her purr bemused.

And Yellow, mischief-maker bold,
Broke a vase, a sight to behold.
Yet, when he sleeps, all's forgiven,
The neighborhood celebrates, truly smitten.

Cat's eye, infallible and keen,
Cat's heart, noble, unseen.
Cat kingdom, a realm unknown,
Will anyone ever uncover its throne?

An Unusual Family

I watch as Grandma knits away,
Golden birds from yarn, they sway.
They can fly, so free and bright,
In flight, they chase fireflies at night.

I see Grandpa, with skilled hand,
Crafting boats from trees, so grand.
Sometimes, in dreams, it seems to me,
They sail down rivers, wild and free.

And then there's Mom, in her domain,
Baking bread, a magical strain.
Sometimes, alas, a mischievous sprite,
Fairies steal her bread at night.

As for Dad, his work's unseen,
Yet he's not idle, as it may seem.
He plants moonbeams with stars so high,
And chats with the moon, under the sky.

Childhood

Childhood, that's the time so sweet,
Where dreams are vast, and trials we meet.
Days are filled with joy and play,
When worries seem so far away.

Every child deserves the right,
To live their childhood, full of light.
To dream, to laugh, to find delight,
And comfort grown-ups with their sight.

Let all the toys come out to play,
For now's the time, without delay.
Let grandparents, too, be prepared,
To stroll with grandkids, showing they cared.

Let the whole world strive to be,
Sharing joy with children free.
May childhood be a peaceful stage,
Before the wisdom of age.

About the Author

Ana S. Gad

Ana S. Gad is the pen name of Ana Stjelja, a Dubai-based, internationally acclaimed writer, editor, journalist, literary translator and digital artist.

In 2005 she graduated from the Faculty of Philology from the Turkish Language and Literature Department. In 2009 she earned a Master's degree in Sufism. In 2012 she obtained her PhD in Literature (with the thesis on the life and work of one of the first Serbian women writers and world travellers Jelena J. Dimitrijević).

She is an award-winning Serbian poet, writer, translator, journalist, independent scientific researcher and editor. She published more than 30 books across various literary genres; the author of numerous research papers and essays on literature, feminism and diverse cultures.

She is the Editor-in-Chief of various online magazines. As an acclaimed and awarded writer, she has published her works in various Serbian and international print and online magazines, literary blogs and portals. In 2018 she established the Association Alia Mundi for Promoting Cultural Diversity. In 2024 she created the "Sands and City Online Magazine: Cultural Pulse of Gulf".

She is a member of the Association of Writers of Serbia, the Association of Journalists of Serbia, the International Federation of Journalists (IFJ) and Europeana – a digital platform and organization that provides access to millions of digitized items from European museums, galleries, libraries, and archives, promoting Europe's cultural heritage.

In 2021, she successfully completed the creative workshop Awake Not Sleeping – Reimagining Fairy Tales for a new generation organized by UN WOMEN for Europe and Central Asia (UN WOMEN ECA) and earned a Certificate of Appreciation. In July 2022, she successfully completed the Introduction to Psychology course at the American Yale University, where her lecturer was the university professor and world-famous (Canadian-American) psychologist Paul Bloom. In November 2023, she successfully completed Culture and Creativity for the Western Balkans programme (CC4WBs), implemented by UNESCO, the British Council and the Italian Agency for Development Cooperation (AICS).

www.ingramcontent.com/pod-product-compliance
Lightning Source LLC
LaVergne TN
LVHW041555070526
838199LV00046B/1987